I AM A WOLF

KELLY LEIGH MILLER

DIAL BOOKS FOR YOUNG READERS

TO MY MOM, DAD, AND ALEXANDER.
THIS BOOK WOULD NOT EXIST
WITHOUT THEIR HELP.
TO FRANKIE, THE ORIGINAL WOLF.

Dial Books for Young Readers
An imprint of Penguin Random House LLC, New York

Visit us online at penguinrandomhouse.com

Library of Congress Cataloging-in-Publication Data
Names: Miller, Kelly Leigh, author, illustrator. | Title: I am a wolf / Kelly Leigh Miller.
Description: New York, NY : Dial Books for Young Readers, [2019] | Summary: "A dog who insists she is a
wolf finds the perfect home with a young girl who sees past her prickly personality"— Provided by publisher.
Identifiers: LCCN 2018040225 | ISBN 9780525553298 (hardback) | Subjects: | CYAC: Dogs—Fiction. | Pet
adoption—Fiction. | BISAC: JUVENILE FICTION / Animals / Dogs. | JUVENILE FICTION / Social Issues /
Emotions & Feelings. | JUVENILE FICTION / Family / Adoption. | Classification: LCC PZ7.1.M5815 Iam 2019
| DDC [E]—dc23 | LC record available at https://lccn.loc.gov/2018040225

Printed in China
1 3 5 7 9 10 8 6 4 2

Design by Jennifer Kelly | Text handlettered by Kelly Leigh Miller
Wolf and all her buddies were drawn digitally!

I AM A WOLF.

I LIVE IN THE WILD.

MOST WOLVES
LIVE IN PACKS...

I'M FINE ON MY OWN.

I AM NOT CUTE.

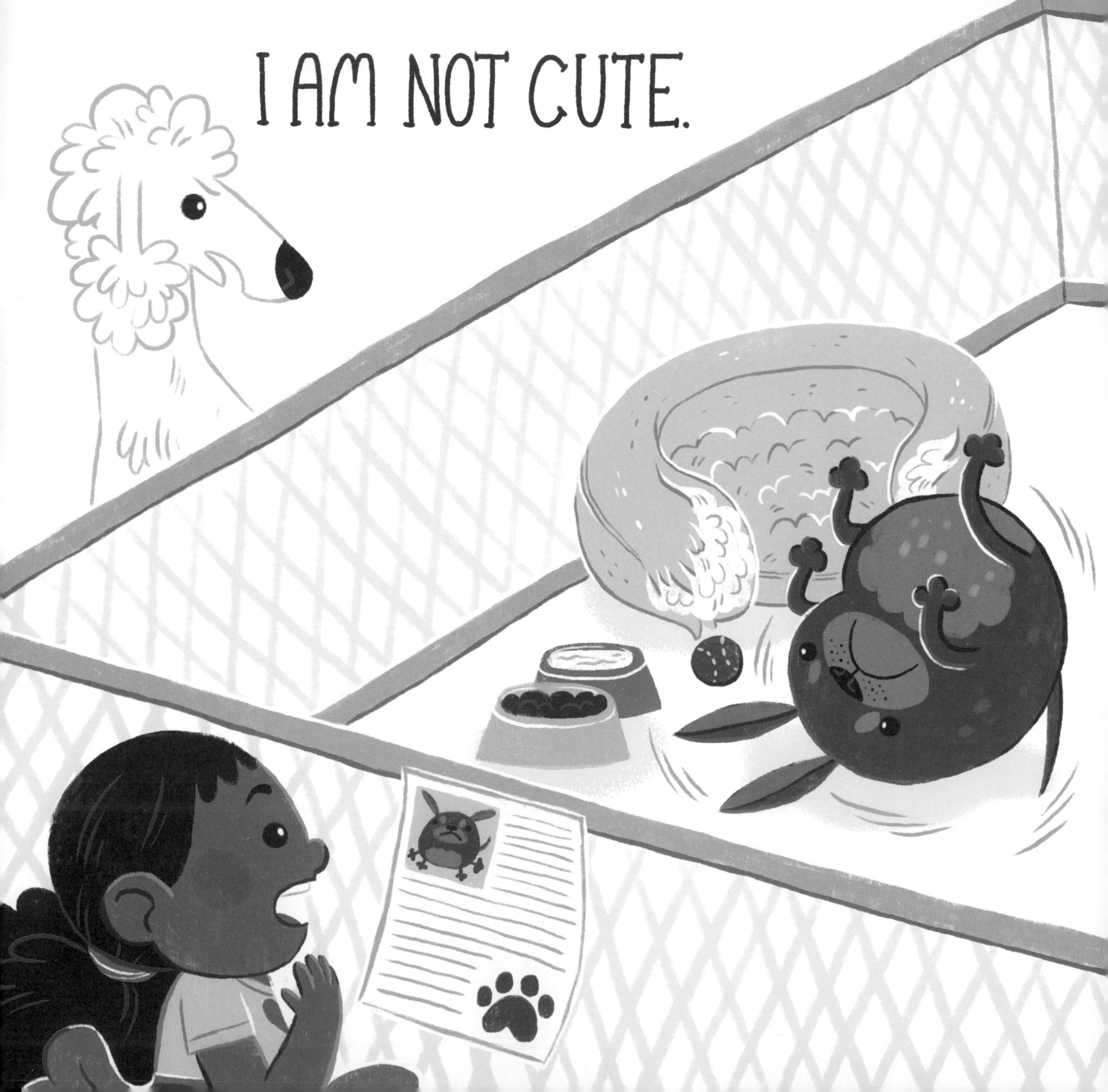

I AM A SCARY BEAST.

I AM A LONE WOLF.

YOU ARE TOO CUTE TO PASS UP!
THE RIGHT FAMILY WILL LOVE YOU!
ANY DAY NOW!
HOW COULD ANYONE NOT ADOPT YOU?

I AM ALONE...

I AM WOLF.

AND THIS IS MY PACK.